A Rookie reader®

I Like Shoes

Written by Candice Ransom
Illustrated by David LaFleur

Children's Press®
A Division of Scholastic Inc.
New York • Toronto • London • Auckland • Sydney
Mexico City • New Delhi • Hong Kong
Danbury, Connecticut

To my sister, who loves shoes more than I do.
— C.R.

For Matisse and Annie, my shoe-loving daughters.
— D.L.

Consultant
Eileen Robinson
Reading Specialist

Library of Congress Cataloging-in-Publication Data

Ransom, Candice F., 1952–
 I like shoes / written by Candice Ransom ;
illustrated by David LaFleur.
     p. cm. — (A Rookie reader)
  Summary: A little girl explains to readers the types of shoes she
likes to wear.
  ISBN 0-516-24858-8 (lib. bdg.)   0-516-25017-5 (pbk.)
  [1. Shoes—Fiction. 2. Stories in rhyme.] I. LaFleur, Dave, ill.
II. Title. III. Series
 PZ8.3.R1467Ial 2005
 [E]—dc22

                    2005003909

CHILDREN'S PRESS and A ROOKIE READER®, and associated logos are trademarks
and or registered trademarks of Scholastic Library Publishing. SCHOLASTIC and
associated logos are trademarks and or registered trademarks of Scholastic Inc.
1 2 3 4 5 6 7 8 9 10 R 14 13 12 11 10 09 08 07 06 05

I like shoes!

Shoes with bows.
Shoes with straps.

Shoes that go tap, tap, tap.

I like flippers.
I like slippers.

I like shoes that close
with zippers.

Shoes that skip.
Shoes that play.

I like shoes that run all day!

Shoes that skate.
Shoes that race.

I like shoes that show my face.

19

Shoes with lights.
Shoes with laces.

I like shoes that take me places!

Word List (28 Words)

(Words in **bold** are story words that rhyme.)

all	I	**play**	**slippers**
bows	**laces**	**race**	**straps**
close	lights	run	take
day	like	shoes	**tap**
face	me	show	that
flippers	my	skate	with
go	**places**	skip	**zippers**

About the Author

Candice Ransom grew up with terrible feet—short, wide, and fat. No shoes fit! She would love to wear pink high-heeled shoes with pointy toes and black silk bows, but usually wears sneakers. They are not very pretty, but they get her from one place to another. Candice is the author of nearly 90 books for children. When she isn't writing, she is working on her scrapbooks or taking dance aerobics classes. She and her husband Frank live in Fredericksburg, Virginia, with their three naughty cats.

About the Illustrator

David LaFleur is an illustrator, designer, and painter serving clients throughout the United States, from his studio in Avon Lake, Ohio. His work has appeared in print ads, on packaging, murals, posters, calendars, shopping bags, books, apparel, and greeting cards.